DRAGONPOX

by Tina Gagliardi   illustrated by Patrick Girouard

Carly's
DRAGON
DAYS

magic
Wagon

visit us at www.abdopublishing.com

Published by Magic Wagon, a division of the ABDO Group, 8000 West 78th Street, Edina, Minnesota 55439.
Copyright © 2009 by Abdo Consulting Group, Inc. International copyrights reserved in all countries. All rights
reserved. No part of this book may be reproduced in any form without written permission from the publisher.

Looking Glass Library™ is a trademark and logo of Magic Wagon.

Printed in the United States.

Text by Tina Gagliardi
Illustrations by Patrick Girouard
Edited by Nadia Higgins and Jill Sherman
Interior layout and design by Nicole Brecke
Cover design by Nicole Brecke

Library of Congress Cataloging-in-Publication Data

Gagliardi, Tina.
 Dragonpox / by Tina Gagliardi ; illustrated by Patrick Girouard.
     p. cm. — (Carly's dragon days)
  ISBN 978-1-60270-594-4
 [1. Dragons—Fiction.] I. Girouard, Patrick, ill. II. Title.
 PZ7.G1242Drd 2009
 [E]—dc22
                                2008035935

Carly was feeling strange. She was so tired she could barely hold her head up. Plus, she had a tickle in her throat that was becoming more and more ticklish.

Gretchen, Carly's imaginary human friend, was worried.

Abigail, the meanest dragon in class, pointed at Carly.

"Eeeeeeeeew," she screamed.

Carly looked down. Her green skin was dotted with bright red spots. Suddenly she felt itchy all over. *Dragonpox!* she thought.

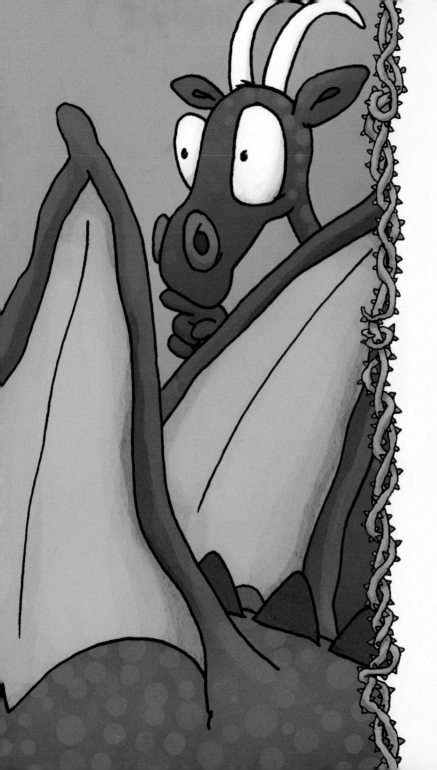

Without warning, Carly coughed. Out came a puff of bright orange smoke.

"Gross!" Abigail shouted. "Mrs. Longhorn!" she called to their teacher. "Make Carly go away!"

"Oh dear," Mrs. Longhorn said when she looked at Carly. "Let's get you to the nurse's office right away."

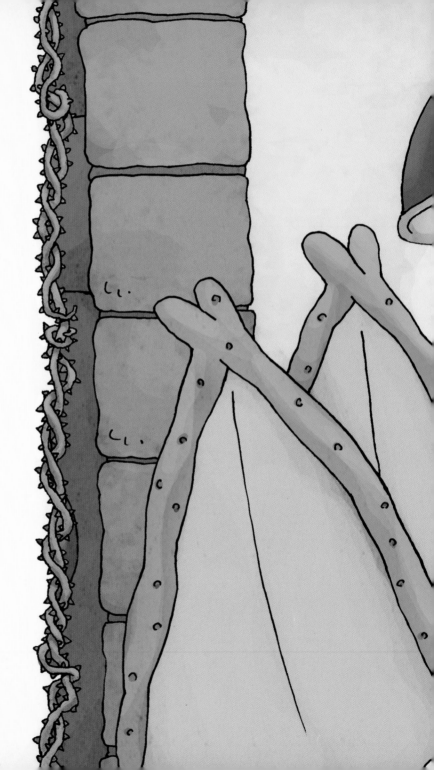

"That's dragonpox, all right!" Nurse Wingtip declared. "You'll need ten days of rest—at least. And remember, do not scratch the red spots!"

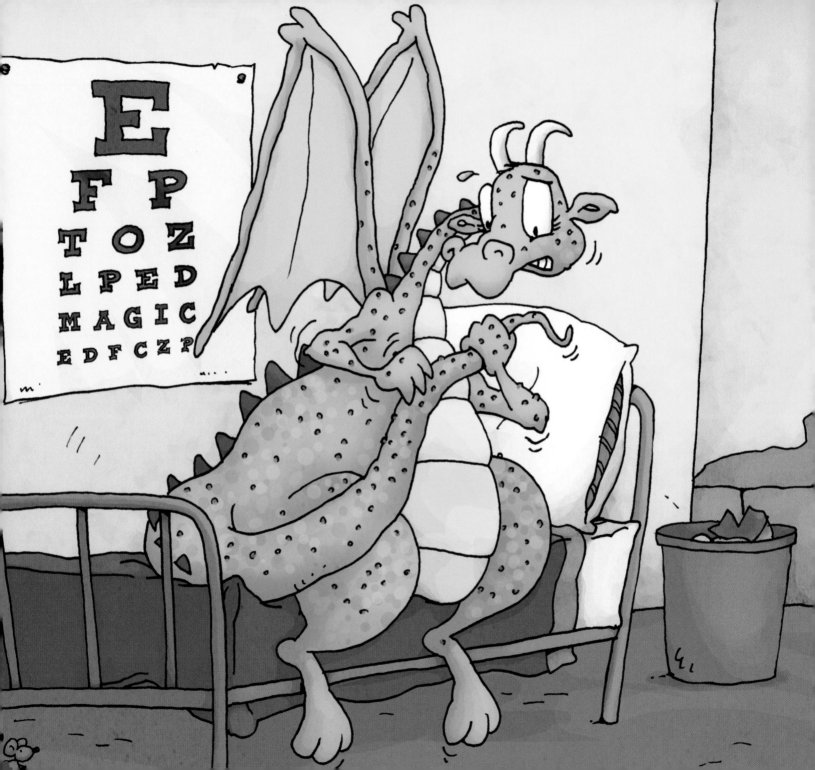

Carly waited for her mom to take her home. Carly tried just pressing on the spots. She tried just blowing on them. She tried everything she could to keep from scratching.

It was no use. Carly ran her claws up and down her tail. "Ahhhhhhhhh," she sighed.

The next day, Carly had even more spots.

Her mom made her an oatmeal bath. "It will help with the itching," she said.

"Yuck!" Carly said, as the oatmeal squished between her claws. She smelled like breakfast for the whole rest of the day.

The day after that, Carly's mom showed up with a big bowl of jiggly green stuff.

"Yay! Jell-O!" Gretchen shouted.

But it turned out to be cucumber lotion.

"Hold still!" Carly's mother ordered, as she rubbed the lotion on Carly's wings. Carly smelled like a salad for the whole rest of the day.

The next morning, Gretchen declared, "I've had it with dragonpox!"

"Me too!" Carly moaned.

"What are we going to do about it?" Gretchen said.

"What do you mean what are we going to do?" Carly said. She still had a week until her ten days of rest were up.

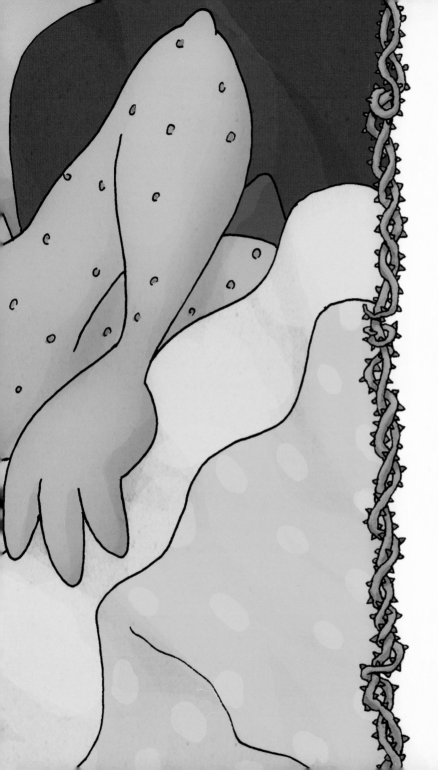

"**O**h, Carly," Gretchen sighed. She hugged her best friend.

"Don't touch me!" Carly warned. "You'll catch it too!"

"No I won't, silly dragon!" Gretchen giggled. "I'm your IMAGINARY friend. I won't get dragonpox unless you IMAGINE I get it."

"Wait a minute!" Gretchen yelled.
"I've got it! I know what to do!"

"What? What?" Carly shouted.

"What if you only have dragonpox in REAL life?" Gretchen said. "But in PRETEND life, you don't?"

"I get it!" Carly shouted. "So in real life I rest and take oatmeal baths and do all the stuff I need to do to get better. But when I'm with you—," Carly began.

"We can do whatever we want!" Gretchen said.

So the next day, while Carly took her oatmeal bath in real life . . .

. . . in pretend life, Carly and Gretchen had brunch with the Queen.

The day after that, while Carly's mom rubbed cucumber lotion on her in real life . . .

. . . Carly and Gretchen invented a cure for boredom.

Before she knew it, Carly was all better. It was time to go back to school.

Carly squeezed into her desk behind Abigail.

In real life, Abigail sneered, "Did your cooties fly away?" . . .

. . . But in pretend life, Carly and Gretchen flew right over Abigail's head, out the door, into the sky, and off to their next great adventure.

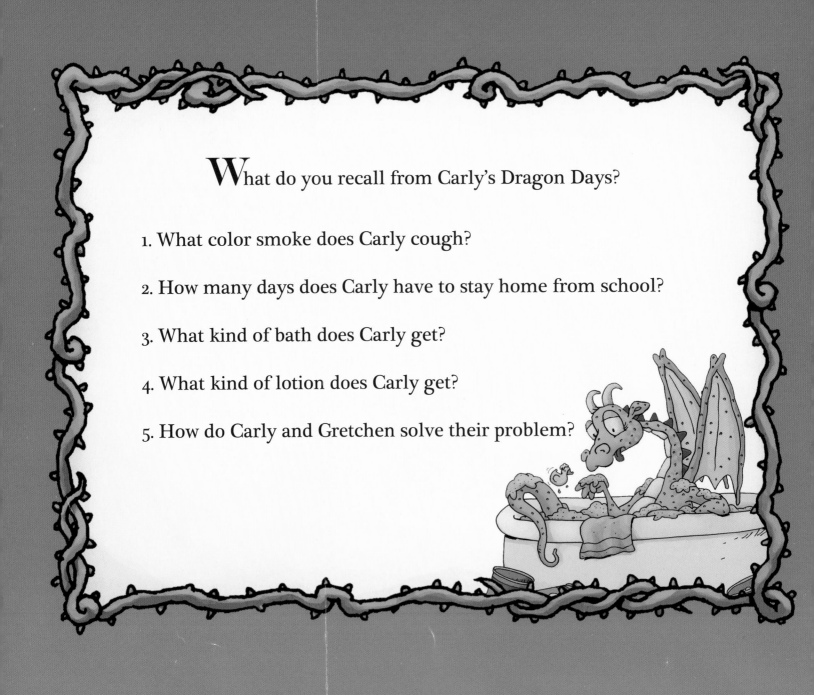

What do you recall from Carly's Dragon Days?

1. What color smoke does Carly cough?

2. How many days does Carly have to stay home from school?

3. What kind of bath does Carly get?

4. What kind of lotion does Carly get?

5. How do Carly and Gretchen solve their problem?

AR 2.4 BL

AR 0.5 PTS

Dragonpox /